Laura Gamsby

For my curious grandmother "Petey"

Little, Brown and Company

Hachette Book Group
237 Park Avenue, New York, NY 10017
Visit our website at www.lb-kids.com

Little, Brown and Company is a division of Hachette Book Group, Inc.
The Little, Brown name and logo are trademarks of Hachette Book Group, Inc.

The publisher is not responsible for websites (or their content) that are not owned by the publisher.

First Edition: April 2009
ISBN 978-0-316-01547-9
20 19 18 17 16 15 14 13 12 11
SC
Manufactured in China

The illustrations for this book were done in acrylic and gouache on board.
The text was set in Mrs Eaves.
Book design by Patti Ann Harris
Printed on recycled paper

PETER BROWN

The Curious Garden

Little, Brown and Company
New York Boston

There once was a city without gardens or
trees or greenery of any kind.
Most people spent their time indoors.
As you can imagine, it was a very dreary place.

However, there was one boy who loved being outside. Even on drizzly days, while everyone else stayed inside, you could always find Liam happily splashing through his neighborhood.

It was on one such morning that Liam made several surprising discoveries. He was wandering around the old railway, as he did from time to time, when he stumbled upon a dark stairwell leading up to the tracks.

The railway had stopped working ages ago.
And since Liam had always wanted to explore the tracks,
there was only one thing for the curious boy to do.

Liam ran up the stairs, pushed open the door, and stepped out onto the railway. The first thing he saw was a lonely patch of color. Wildflowers and plants were the last things he had expected to find up there. But when he took a closer look, it became clear that the plants were dying. They needed a gardener.

Liam may not have been a gardener, but he knew that he could help. So he returned to the railway the very next day and got to work. The flowers nearly drowned and he had a few pruning problems, but the plants patiently waited while Liam found better ways of gardening.

As the weeks rolled by, Liam began to feel like a real gardener,
and the plants began to feel like a real garden.

Most gardens stay in one place. But this was no ordinary garden. With miles of open railway ahead of it, the garden was growing restless. It wanted to explore.

The tough little weeds and mosses were the first to move. They popped up farther and farther down the tracks and were closely followed by the more delicate plants.

Over the next few months, Liam and the curious
garden explored every corner of the railway.

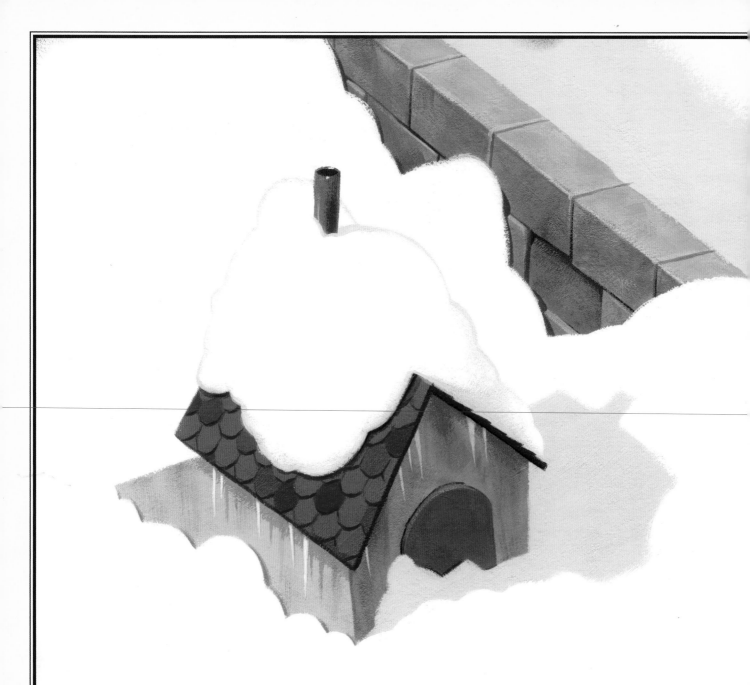

After spending his spring and summer and autumn with the garden, Liam's time on the railway was finally interrupted by winter. Heavy blankets of snow fell on the city that season. And for the first time since he'd become a gardener, Liam could not visit the plants.

Rather than waste his winter worrying about the garden,
Liam spent it preparing for spring.

After three cold months the snow finally began to melt, and Liam rolled his new gardening gear over to the railway.

Winter had taken a toll on the garden.

But thanks to Liam's planning, his handy new tools,
and a little help from the sun, the plants soon awoke
from their winter sleep.

The garden had always wanted to explore the rest of the city, and that spring it was finally ready to make its move. Once again, the tough little weeds and mosses set out first. They popped up farther and farther from the railway and were closely followed by the more delicate plants.

The garden was especially curious about old,
forgotten things.

A few plants popped up where they didn't belong.

Others mysteriously popped up all at once.

But the most surprising things that popped up were the new gardeners.

Many years later, the entire
city had blossomed. But of all
the new gardens, Liam's favorite
was where it all began.

Author's Note:

It often seems impossible for nature to thrive in a city of concrete and brick and steel. But the more I've traveled, and the closer I've looked at the world around me, the more I've realized that nature is always eagerly exploring the places we've forgotten. You can find flowers and fields and even small forests growing wild in every city; you just have to look for them.

On the west side of Manhattan there is an old, elevated railway called the High Line. Its trains rumbled high above the city streets for decades, but in 1980 the High Line was shut down and forgotten. Without people and trains getting in the way, nature was free to redecorate. Over the years, the rusty rails and gravel slowly gave way to wildflowers and trees. And if you look at the railway today you'll see a lush garden that curves above the streets and between buildings.

From grass bursting through cracks in a sidewalk, or a tuft of goldenrod clinging to a brick wall, to a meadow winding along an abandoned railway, nature can thrive in the unlikeliest of places.

All of this made me curious: what would happen if an entire city decided to truly cooperate with nature? How would that city change? How would it all begin?

Peter Brown